D1106874

Dear Parent:

Congratulations! Your child is taking the first steps on an exciting journey. The destination? Independent reading!

STEP INTO READING® will help your child get there. The program offers five steps to reading success. Each step includes fun stories and colorful art. There are also Step into Reading Sticker Books, Step into Reading Math Readers, Step into Reading Phonics Readers, Step into Reading Write-In Readers, and Step into Reading Phonics Boxed Sets—a complete literacy program with something to interest every child.

Learning to Read, Step by Step!

Ready to Read   Preschool–Kindergarten
• big type and easy words • rhyme and rhythm • picture clues
For children who know the alphabet and are eager to begin reading.

Reading with Help   Preschool–Grade 1
• basic vocabulary • short sentences • simple stories
For children who recognize familiar words and sound out new words with help.

Reading on Your Own   Grades 1–3
• engaging characters • easy-to-follow plots • popular topics
For children who are ready to read on their own.

Reading Paragraphs   Grades 2–3
• challenging vocabulary • short paragraphs • exciting stories
For newly independent readers who read simple sentences with confidence.

Ready for Chapters   Grades 2–4
• chapters • longer paragraphs • full-color art
For children who want to take the plunge into chapter books but still like colorful pictures.

STEP INTO READING® is designed to give every child a successful reading experience. The grade levels are only guides. Children can progress through the steps at their own speed, developing confidence in their reading, no matter what their grade.

Remember, a lifetime love of reading starts with a single step!

Thomas the Tank Engine & Friends ™ CREATED BY BRITT ALLCROFT

Based on the Railway Series by the Reverend W Awdry
© 2017 Gullane (Thomas) LLC. Thomas the Tank Engine & Friends and Thomas & Friends
are trademarks of Gullane (Thomas) Limited.
Thomas the Tank Engine & Friends and Design Is Reg. U.S. Pat. and Tm. Off.
© 2017 HIT Entertainment Limited.
All rights reserved. Published in the United States by Random House Children's Books,
a division of Penguin Random House LLC, 1745 Broadway, New York, NY 10019, and in
Canada by Penguin Random House Canada Limited, Toronto.
Step into Reading, Random House, and the Random House colophon are registered
trademarks of Penguin Random House LLC.

Visit us on the Web!
StepIntoReading.com
randomhousekids.com
www.thomasandfriends.com

Educators and librarians, for a variety of teaching tools, visit us at
RHTeachersLibrarians.com

ISBN 978-0-399-55862-7 (trade) — ISBN 978-0-399-55863-4 (lib. bdg.)

Printed in the United States of America
10 9 8 7 6 5 4 3 2 1
Random House Children's Books supports the First Amendment and
celebrates the right to read.

HIT entertainment

THOMAS & FRIENDS™

Henry in the Dark

Based on the Railway Series by the Reverend W Awdry

Random House 🏠 New York

Henry needs
new paint.

He goes to
the Steamworks.

Henry gets painted.

It is the wrong paint.

Now he glows
in the dark!

Thomas sees
Henry.
He thinks Henry
is a ghost!
Henry does not
know why.

James sees Henry.
He thinks Henry
is a ghost.

Henry does not
know why.

Gordon sees Henry.

He thinks Henry
is a ghost!

The engines
stay in the sheds.

They are scared
of the ghost!

Cranky sees Henry.

He thinks Henry

is a ghost.

Henry does not

know why.

Then Henry sees
his new paint.
He is glowing!

Sir Topham Hatt
sees Henry.
He thinks Henry
is a ghost!

Now Henry

knows why.

Gordon sees that
the ghost is Henry.

James sees that
the ghost is Henry.

Only Henry
has done his work.
Sir Topham Hatt
is pleased.
Henry is happy!